Dream On, Dancing Queen

Chloe Laube

Andrew Benzie Books
Walnut Creek, California

Published by Andrew Benzie Books
www.andrewbenziebooks.com

Printed in the United States of America

First Edition: December 2015

10 9 8 7 6 5 4 3 2 1

Laube, Chloe
Dream On, Dancing Queen

ISBN: 978-1-941713-28-0

Cover design and book design by Andrew Benzie

Dream On, Dancing Queen enjoys a five-star rating on Amazon.

Amazon reviews:

A RARE FIND

This compelling book is a rare combination of sassy and poignant, hilarious and tragic—so well-written you want to reread passages and savor the words. The story will break your heart as you laugh out loud and the ending is so satisfying, and so clever, you want to read it over and over.

SAD AND FUNNY AT THE SAME TIME

Chloe Laube's writing is eloquent. The story is romantic, sad, and funny all at the same time. I could not put it down. Kudos to Ms. Laube! Can't wait for her next adventure!

A COMPELLING READ

This is a compelling, authentic story that is both gripping and cathartic. The prose is taught and the ending a surprise. Everyone needs a "Josie" in their life; a straight shooter all the way. What compels the reader forward (and while holding your breath) are thoughts of 'uh oh, now it comes'… and it does not…

A LITERARY STAR IS BORN

I found this book riveting—I couldn't put it down and read it in one sitting! Ms. Laube doesn't waste a word in weaving her intriguing tale. I particularly loved her clever, sardonic wit and will be recommending the book to everyone I know.

FIVE STARS

Brilliant! Funny. A cautionary tale.

25th Annual Writer's Digest
Self-Published Book Awards
Judges Commentary:

Dream On, Dancing Queen, by Chloe Laube is a tiny book that has it all. Fun and funny, the little volume is also a bit sad and scary. With economy of words and pages, Laube has delivered a top-notch tale that includes travel, glamour, fun and mayhem. There is not a missed beat to be found on any page. The size of the book might be off putting for some who typically read weightier volumes, but the size is perfect for the tale within. There is not a wasted word nor a need for one more.

To you, my love.

The Dancing Queen Awakens

My shrink tells me to always make "I" statements. Well, here goes.

I despise you.

Let me tell you why. You lied, deceived, and betrayed me. I loved you, and you manipulated that love into a tortured emotional hell.

Anger stains the remembrance of every beautiful moment we shared. I was 65 years old when we met (well—maybe 68, but a mini-lift had worked wonders) and my heart had been deprived far too long.

My first marriage, which I foolishly thought would last forever, was dissolved 20 years before. My husband screwed every secretary on the corporate ladder to climb another rung.

I was too bedazzled with him to know anything was wrong until the laundry came out pink one day, and I found a lacey red thong stuffed in the pocket of his sweatshirt. He also stashed most of our assets, and the law was indifferent to his infidelities, so I ended up divorced, thirty-four years old, with $7,000 to my name.

Sure, a few flings followed, some fun, some hot, some not, but I wasn't cut out for casual coupling. I needed one man to love. One worthy man.

The need for economic survival prevailed over the longings of my heart, so I slaved for 33 years at a social service agency more dysfunctional than the DMV. Josie Wong was my first supervisor, also a neophyte, and we endured the madhouse, clinging to one another like lost little children in mutual fear of a diabolical alcoholic manager.

We were an unlikely duo. Josie, first generation Chinese, was short and plump (she claimed to be five feet, but I seemed six inches taller at five-four). We both wore petite sizes, and she could never figure out why, at my immense height, I wore size six and she wore size twelve.

She was also fiercely defiant.

"In my next life, I will be rich, tall, and willowy, have the grace of a ballerina, and cut off the balls of that stupid ass we work for," she snorted. His balls remained intact in this life but shriveled to dried prunes when he was demoted, and Josie grabbed his job two years later.

I, on the other hand, was Caucasian, slender, blonde, and by nature a trusting conciliator, noted for my tact and quiet finesse. Josie referred to me as a greenhorn gringo and was always on the alert to protect me from my own gullibility.

Every few years we treated ourselves to a cruise to gather the energy to complete our civil service indenture. Knowing we would eventually smack into the glass ceiling, we carefully calculated pensions and savings. When our heads hit that barrier with a thud, we had ample resources to further explore the enticements of the world.

But then my mother fell ill. Josie stood watch while I, childless and an only child, tended to Mom as lung cancer crawled up into her brain and ate it cell by cell.

"The beasts arc wild today. That tigcr is undcr your chair right now, and it just bit off your bad foot," Mom would say, trying to swat it and shoo the lions away.

She thought she was shackled in iron boots because she could no longer move her legs. "Take these things off me. They're worse than the ones you had when you were paralyzed. Get me out of here."

She screamed a lot. Hate poured from her once loving eyes, and I could only spend a few minutes at the nursing home before her rage would erupt.

My poor little mom died an awful death, and six months later, I was still stunned by the gruesome hallucinations and twisted perceptions she endured, all of which could have been ended with one merciful act, but Hospice doesn't work that way.

Josie finally intervened with a proposal that overcame my lingering grief and depression. The two of us had taken dance lessons for years, she to overcome an innate clumsiness, and I to overcome the weakness in my right leg, the result of polio at age five.

My childhood had been a nightmare of partial paralysis, iron braces, frightening surgeries, and isolation—who knew where that evil virus came from or if it was still lurking inside me, ready to jump out on the next kid who came by?

I finally escaped the orthopedic terrorists and was fairly together by adulthood, hindered primarily by a fused right ankle that made it almost impossible to walk on uneven surfaces without tearing apart my knee.

When Josie invited me to a party at the dance studio where she had begun taking lessons, I was astounded that she could waltz around seemingly at ease. Not one yelp of pain was emitted by her instructor when she scrunched his instep.

"Try it," she urged. "I think you can do it."

"I can't tell a rhumba from a cha-cha, and what if I fall?"

"Then you can sue—but not until I've used up all the lessons I've paid for."

So, I gave it a shot and a hardwood floor became a safe and joyful haven.

Our current instructor, Alex, was perfect for me, because he had been a dancer in a theatrical group until a scaffolding on stage had collapsed with him on it. His right leg was fractured almost to dust, and it had been glued and pinioned back together.

He learned to fake, adjust, and revise almost every move and taught me how to compensate for the lack of movement in my right ankle. With his encouragement, I fancied myself a dancing queen despite my limp.

*　　　*　　　*

"Look at this," Josie said, shoving a glossy brochure under my nose. "The Star Sapphire is sailing from Barcelona September 19th, and it's the last Mediterranean cruise they're doing this year. And look who's dance hosting."

The more elite cruise lines engaged the services of cultivated gentlemen to dance with unescorted ladies—and the women aboard loved to dress to the hilt and float around the floor with courtly men, secure in the knowledge that the hosts were carefully screened, and seedy predators had been weeded out. Handsome, well-mannered opportunists were another story.

My heart jumped when I looked at the brochure. Jon De Grout's sly, seductive face was featured on page four—a prized, preening dancer who ruled the seas with his ballroom expertise.

We'd been on three cruises where he had managed to convince every single woman on board that she was "the one" while he remained impossibly aloof. I needed no further prodding.

"Okay, I'm in. Will you book the reservations?" I asked.

"Already did. Better get your hair done, take a few lessons, and start packing."

Alex was flabbergasted when I called.

"You want me to bring you up to an advanced level in three weeks? I'm a dance instructor, not a magician."

"Well, we can try, can't we?" I pleaded.

By the time Josie and I flew into Barcelona on the 17th I had perfected the feather step in the Foxtrot, and my Cuban motion made the most of my meager rear.

Josie and I took the city bus tour from our hotel twice to drink in the incredibly fanciful and inspiring creations of Gaudi, Spain's most famous architect. We were awed by his Sagrada Familia, a basilica with spires defying gravity and intended to eventually touch the clouds.

We strolled down La Ramblas, Barcelona's legendary boulevard paved with weaving tiles, flanked by innumerable tapas bars and kiosks filled with flowers and cages holding colorful little singing birds. It took a while for us to realize that the many costumed statues along the way were actually people, trained to hold a position with no movement, not even their eyes, for literally hours.

We were scared spitless when we realized that we had wandered way past the part prettied up for tourists and took a taxi to the pier to avoid being mugged or kidnapped.

*   *   *

Our delicate, elegant ship, the Sapphire, was wedged between two Norwegian vessels—bloated floating cities, each crammed with thirty-five hundred passengers desperate to traverse the two miles from stateroom to dining room in less than half a day. One third of them would be single women vying for the attention of any male not holding hands with another male.

Josie too, had been derailed by divorce in her mid- thirties. The hit to my heart was an emotional devastation, but Josie, who didn't like her husband ("up-tight little chink," she called him) was outraged by the division of property and the outlay of cash required to buy him out of their house to keep a roof over her head.

An annoying parade of balding, bearded, barrel-bellied suitors had turned me off, and Josie was still grousing about her divorce payout twenty years ago, so we were not seeking romance when we boarded the Sapphire. We wanted ballroom bliss and Jon, the master dancer, could provide it.

*   *   *

The late seating worked best for us, so we would have time to put ourselves together after the day's happenings. I changed into black crepe pants and a sparkling top before dinner, hoping to catch Jon's eye without overdoing it, and we went directly to the Stardust dance theater after dinner, dance shoes tucked in our bags.

The hosts always sat in the raised back area so they could spot the unescorted ladies easily. A few brazen women would join the hosts in back, but Josie and I always sat in the front row, right next to the dance floor, playing a form of hard to get, I suppose.

The lighting was dim, nightclub style, and when the band, straight from Manila began to play, I felt a presence behind me.

"Would you care to dance?" I turned in my chair expecting to see Jon.

Not so. It was you, and you exclaimed, with surprise, "You're so pretty!"

I couldn't believe my eyes. You were ruggedly handsome: six feet tall, broad shouldered, perfect posture, Roman nose, blue eyes, straight white hair.

Nor could I believe my heart, long dormant, fluttering to life.

I offered you my hand, and you led me onto the dance floor. I looked up, you looked down, our eyes locked, and I knew you felt it too—an overpowering connection, not just sensual or sexual but something much deeper, a primal feeling of belonging.

Once your arms were around me, I knew that's where I wanted to be—forever. We swept into a waltz, rose and fell, whirled and twirled, and neither of us needed to say a word. We were in perfect harmony.

"What's your name?" You asked as you led me back to my chair. The brass tag attached to the pocket of your dark blue blazer read, "Nick Romano, Sapphire Host."

"Cara. Cara Farrar. And Nick stands for what?"

"Dominic. My parents emigrated from Italy, and my mother refused to give any of her kids Italian names. I was fifth, the last, and my father finally put his foot down. Otherwise, I would have been named Oscar."

"Whatever you do, Cara, don't jump ship," you said, squeezing my hand.

"Now I have to tackle a couple of these eighteen-wheelers," you mumbled, your eyes scanning the dance floor.

I had no idea what you were talking about until you walked over to a huge, glowering Hungarian woman who was keeping tabs on how the dance rotation was going. All six hosts were obliged to change partners every dance to make sure a little stardust was sprinkled about for every lady.

Two dances later, Jon greeted me effusively and cha-cha'd as if his pants were on fire. (Third timers were entitled to a bit more attention, but not to more dances—the Hungarian women were scarier than the Captain's rules.)

No matter. I bided my time, knowing that my turn would come. Josie would get restless after an hour or so and take off for the casino, but I stayed until the end.

The Manila Boys band packed up their instruments at exactly 12:30 because they only had fifteen minutes to change into waiters' gear and run up to the Lido deck to clear the carnage left from the midnight buffet.

Within a minute, Jon was at my side and extended his arm. I was quite flattered, thinking he was going to escort me to a lounge for a drink, but instead, he led me to the elevator and wished me safe passage to Deck #8. I had no choice but to step into the mirrored box, so there was no nightcap with him, and worse yet, no chance for one with you.

*   *   *

I think the ship's first port was at Toulon, France, but I have no recollection of the town or any excursion, if there was one. I was smitten with you almost to the point of obsession.

Next came Monaco, its fairy-tale harbor filled with rich peoples' yachts, and floating empires, roofed by helicopter pads, belonging to Arabian sheiks. The Prince's palace was shabby, and so was the Casino de Monte Carlo, more Reno than Las Vegas. Josie was miffed that she had to dress up and wear real shoes just to get in the door.

"Tacky joint. Let's split," she said, and we did. Back to the ship to gussy up for the Captain's Welcoming Party. I wore my best black gown, slim, floor length, with long lacey sleeves and the hint of a train.

It must have worked, because you chose me for the first dance, and I felt as royal as Princess Grace. Champagne flowed, and at dinner, I only ate two olives and one scoop of caviar so I would be feather light for the evening dance.

I approached the Stardust Room somewhat light-headed due to the Captain's champagne and lack of food, but what I saw snapped me into a state of alarm.

The scene had changed. A woman named Estelle had inserted herself into the hosts' row. She had long, over-bleached hair, a big laugh, and big implants. Her too tight dress exposed a lot of cleavage and a bountiful rear. Uh-oh.

But the magic with you hadn't changed. Pure joy overtook us on the dance floor, and I showered you with smiles while you enticed me with flirtatious murmurs. Then you moved on to the grim Hungarians, cloying Estelle, and the rest of the lineup.

The Manila Boys would eventually play taps. Not really—it was always a dreary, *Good Night, Sweetheart*, as Jon would grasp my elbow, and I would be exiled to Deck #8. Jon kept herding me like a border collie rounding up a stray sheep to return to its pen, and I had no idea why he was doing this.

I came somewhat to my senses in Florence, on the Ponte Vecchio. Hundreds of fine jewelry shops lined the narrow bridge crossing the Arno River, and all that gold aroused a different type of lust.

Josie and I jostled with the Japanese and Germans for peeks at bangles worth more than our houses, and then we crossed the river at three different points trying to find Stefanatti's majolica studio to buy one of his beautiful ceramic pieces. The Duomo was undergoing a major restoration, half-covered in scaffolding, but that was the only disappointment in that beautiful little city.

I almost forgot that I had seen you having breakfast with Estelle before we left the ship for the day. She was leaning over the table to maximize her silicone exposure, but you appeared more into your eggs benedict, accompanied by a pile of country fried potatoes and bacon. A sign was propped up by your table, which meant you were leading a group on a tour bus—another function of hosts, if they chose.

Next up was Rome, and a taxi took Josie and me to every sight in the tour book in the six hours we had to spend ashore. Years before, the four-mile trek through the Vatican had been too much for my knee, and I was covered with bruises inflicted by rude tourists shoving and swinging 30-pound backpacks. I wanted more than anything to go inside the Colosseum, but the tour book warned that walking was difficult, so the taxi was fine.

We sailed on, and Sorrento rose majestically from the sea, its massive cliffs shored by walls the Romans had built. Another bit of disappointment, because the major shore tour was to Pompeii, but again, the tour book warned of very difficult walking, so I didn't go.

The ship made a little jog to Mykonos, an island from an ancient time that could still be felt, all buildings painted a dazzling white, streets twisted into mazes designed to confuse marauding pirates, and a relentless sun blazing at 116 degrees. That's the place that should have had a warning in the tour book.

As soon as we got back to the ship, I hobbled up the gangplank to our stateroom and started filling the bathtub with cold water.

"Josie, my feet are so swollen, I'll have to sit in this ice water for two hours to get into my dance shoes tonight. Time is running out. We've only got a stop at Dubrovnic, and then one last day and night in Venice."

"Fuck Nick," Josie spit out.

"That's sort of what I had in mind, but he doesn't seem too responsive," I replied.

"Exactly. And every female on this ship thinks

you've got something going with Jon. Be careful on deck and don't go near the railing if you see a Hungarian."

"Maybe Nick thinks I have a thing with Jon, and that's why he's not making any moves."

"Dream on, dancing queen."

*   *   *

Well, if I didn't find a way to distinguish myself on the next stop, Estelle could bop around with abandon. Josie was right, and I was through mooning.

Dubrovnic is a medieval walled city with steps that would have demolished my knee, and I did not want the services of a Croatian orthopedist.

Instead, we took an overland tour. Three buses were lined up on the dock, and you were one of three hosts standing by with guide signs. We had to board in order of arrival, so Josie and I were put on the first bus and yours was the last.

The countryside was dotted with olive trees, and the trip ended at a sprawling inn. The buses were too big to get into the parking lot, so we got off and walked up a wooded path next to a stream with real paddlewheels and pools filled with jumping fish.

Picnic tables were spread out in a clearing with plates piled with local cheeses, prosciutto, olives, and many bottles of homemade wine.

When the last bus arrived and all the people were seated, there was only one place left on one of the benches. I saw you, the last person off the last bus, coming up the path.

"Josie, could you scoot over a little so we could make room for Nick?" I asked. She promptly moved closer to me.

"No, I meant the other way so Nick could sit between us."

"Shit. Then I'll be smashed up against the Hungarian," she hissed.

"Then let's trade places."

"What's in it for me?" she asked.

"My pastry."

We transferred plastic glasses, paper plates, and ourselves, quickly making a nice little space, and the Hungarian jabbed her elbow into my ribs.

You got to the top of the path, looked around, walked over, and squeezed in between Josie and me. I swear the chemistry crackled between us when your perfect butt hit the bench, but that wasn't going to be enough to override Estelle's frontage. I had to make an indelible impression with two thirds less volume.

"Buon Giorno, Josie and Cara. My bus was late. Not much food left." You sighed, with a hangdog look. Josie stuffed my entire cream puff into her mouth.

I'd seen what you consumed less than two hours ago, and I realized that the key to the kingdom of Dominic had been placed in my hand. You loved food.

"I've got all this cheese and prosciutto left, and I don't want to turn into an eighteen-wheeler. Please take it," I said.

You looked like a puppy with its first Milkbone. "Wouldn't want that to happen, little one. Thanks," you said, as you pounced on my leftovers. Then you hopped back over the bench, gave my shoulder an affectionate squeeze, and picked up your sign.

"Got to go round up and count heads now. Once they get into the wine, they forget about the bus and leave half their gear. See you tonight. First Rhumba is mine."

My heart leapt. At last, a breakthrough, and it would be smooth sailing to Venice.

Wrong.

*   *   *

Estelle was in full bloom that evening at the Captain's Farewell Gala, her assets prominently highlighted by plunging red satin.

"If she tries a Samba, those balloons are going to pop out. I wonder if they float," Josie speculated.

I was really galled when Estelle cornered the ship's photographer to have her picture taken with all six hosts. Then you motioned for Josie and me to join in, and the photographer arranged the group by height.

Josie was the shortest, and her grinning face obliterated Estelle's cleavage. Estelle pouted like a teenage brat, and Jon, anticipating an unseemly incident, warned the Manila Boys to avoid playing Sambas and Salsas for the evening.

Dance after dance, and no invitation—not even for a cappuccino. Once again, I was exiled to Deck #8 with Jon steering my elbow, and I could hear Estelle yacking it up with gusto with the rest of the hosts.

Josie and I woke up early the next morning, our last day in Venice. The ships had to dock far from the city, so we boarded tenders (the small boats suspended from the ship and intended for both transport and/or rescue) and swept down the Grand Canal, passing beautiful, once palatial buildings, now faded and gradually sinking into the water.

We splashed by the Doges Palace and the Bridge of Sighs, but I couldn't take the tour because of the steps. No matter: I loved all of Venice.

Josie and I took a gondola ride through the backwaters, saw a submerging house where Marco Polo purportedly lived (I didn't think so), and entertained ourselves in St. Mark's Square, window-shopping and watching the pigeons outwit the café waiters to snatch up crumbs.

Then we went back to the dock where water taxis, gondola's, and the local waterbuses cluster, spent the rest of the day hopping on and off the local waterbuses, and reluctantly took the last tender back to the ship.

"I'm not going to dance tonight," Josie announced. "I have too much to pack (she had to buy two extra suitcases to hold all the stuff she'd bought), and we have to disembark at 4:30 a.m."

Well, this would be my last shot, and the dance

would end early, at 12:00, to accommodate early departures. I packed everything except my travel clothes, and because I couldn't compete with Estelle's cleavage, I wore a black silk mock-turtleneck top with flared tango pants to dinner.

But the situation was dire. Since Josie wasn't going to the dance, she relinquished the bathroom to me to primp at leisure, and I went for it. I styled my blond, cap-like hair so that my bangs fell seductively (I hoped) to one side. My arsenal of Clinique's beauty aids transformed my hazel eyes to almond-shaped pools, my skin to soft peach, my cheeks to glowing pink, my eyelids to shimmering silver, and my lips to lush watermelon. I was looking good!

I waited from 8:30 to 11:50 for you to say something—anything, other than the usual banter. And at precisely 11:51, you asked me for a Foxtrot, and murmured halfway through, "Will you have a drink with me in the Avenue Saloon?"

I kept my cool and hesitated at least five seconds before I said, "Yes. I'd like that."

"We've got a logistics problem here," you whispered. "You need to ditch Jon and I have to escape Estelle. You leave right now and hide in a ladies' room until ten after twelve. I know a back way to the Saloon, so I'll meet you there."

You danced us over to an exit, squeezed my hand, and gave me a little push out the door.

Was this it?

*   *   *

It was.

The Avenue Saloon was small, dark, and plush, the most out-of-the-way bar on the ship and originally designed to hide cigar smokers. You were already seated on a plumped-up love seat, and when I sat down, I sank into the cushions and you.

We sat wedged thigh to thigh and Ricky, the waiter who manned the gelato station in the afternoon, came over and asked us what we wanted to drink. "Scotch on the rocks," you said, and I asked for a glass of zinfandel.

"Do you think Jon's going to look for me?" I asked.

"No. I told him Estelle had big plans for him for the evening, so he split to hide out in the gym. What a schmuck. He whisked you away every night to spite me because he knows I like you."

I detected a bit of envy, perhaps because Jon was always designated by the Captain to escort the richest single woman aboard to the last gala. Ricky returned with our drinks, and you looked quizzically at the lush red contents of my glass.

"I thought zinfandel was pink," you said.

"Well, some of it is, but no one within a hundred miles of Napa or Sonoma would drink it. What's a schmuck?"

"Questo e' tutto! That explains your accent. You're from California—and a schmuck is a colossal ass."

I didn't think Californians had an accent, but you sure did.

"Do I hear Brooklyn?" I asked.

"Yep. My parents were straight off the boat from Italy. They actually met while being processed on Ellis Island. My father grubbed for work in the garment district. We were dirt poor and lived over a pool hall in the Italian ghetto right next to the Jewish quarter. So, I picked up English and Yiddish from the street."

"I've heard you spattering dabs of French, Spanish, and German to the passengers and staff."

"Always had an ear for languages. Is that wine any good?"

"Excellent. Full of raspberry and cherry. Want a taste?"

"Okay."

I handed him the glass, and he took a cautious sip.

"What do you think of it?" I asked.

"Sure beats Manischewits, but I don't taste any fruit."

"It takes a little time to develop the taste buds. See the little legs running down the inside of the glass?"

"Yeah."

"That tells you it is a very well-crafted wine. So, where did the Spanish, French, and German come from?" I asked.

"Well, all the Italian kids went to Catholic school, my father terrified me into getting good grades, and I was athletic. St. John's was a fancy prep school and desperate for a winning baseball team, so the parish priest pulled some strings, and I got a full scholarship. Took Spanish and French because they were easy for me, and I played a lot of baseball."

"And the German?"

"I love to ski. France, Germany, wherever the snow is the best. That's why I live in Sun Valley now."

"I took four years of high school Latin, two years of Italian at Berkeley, and all I remember is *un po di zucchero*, which had something to do with sugar, as I recall," I said.

You burst out laughing, and then said, "We'll fix that."

"Were you ever married?" I had to ask, hoping the past tense was correct.

"Once. I was twenty-two. Right after I graduated from Brooklyn College, my girlfriend got pregnant. Before I knew it, we were married and had two kids. What a disaster. Not the kids, the babies were my heart, but my wife was mean as hell.

"I landed a job in the Bronx teaching PE, and after the divorce, I had to pay child support, so weekends I managed a ski lodge and later on I landed a job with a vacation flight company. That's how I got to ski at all the ritzy slopes in Europe. Not a bad deal, if you have to moonlight. Enough about me. Let's talk about you."

Oh, God. Here was this cosmopolitan man of the world, with his pick of rich dowagers in the penthouse suites, and he wanted to know about quiet, not rich, not voluptuous, not fascinating me.

"Well, I was married once to a very ambitious man who put his career ahead of everything else. I was a social worker at a group home for runaways and loved my job. My husband got a job offer in Chicago, accepted it without even asking me, sold the house we had just bought, sold my little Volkswagen because it wasn't grand enough, and moved us to a Chicago high rise on the Gold Coast.

"I was a prisoner, and the life of a corporate wife wasn't for me, so I moved back to California, divorced and started all over."

That was enough history for the moment. You were 72 and I was 68. We had 140 years of life to explore: books, movies, families, travels, favorite places. You couldn't believe how little I had seen domestically.

"Not even the Rockies, the Grand Canyon, Mt. Rushmore?"

I shook my head. "No."

"Wait until I show you New Mexico, Arizona, Utah—unbelievable beauty."

I was stunned. You actually wanted to see more of me.

When Ricky kicked us out at 3:00 am, you said you would be in touch as soon as you got home—sometime in late October, because you were under contract for another voyage.

You held my hand and walked me to the elevator, and then you hugged me tightly, raised my hand and kissed it. I adored you, and I knew I wanted you by my side, holding my hand, for the rest of my life.

I staggered, love-drunk, past hundreds of suitcases lining the corridor and into Stateroom 840.

Josie was sitting on the edge of her bed.

"My God, what happened? Where were you? You know we have to be out of here in one hour," she said, and then she gave me a piercing look.

"Did you go to bed with Nick?" she asked.

"Nope. Even better. We just talked for three hours, and I think we have fallen in love," I said.

"Jesus, are you nuts? He's a dance host gigolo!"

"Maybe so, maybe not. But I know he's my man."

*　　　*　　　*

And you were.

I left the ship filled with longing and hope. October was going to be the longest month I had ever endured, and Josie wasn't much help.

"Casanova is not going to come to Clayton, California on a mission to woo you. He's spent six months out of each of the last seven years dancing up filthy rich women—and he's taken full advantage of open invitations to dozens of penthouse suites."

"How do you know that?"

"I have my resources." She looked smug and very sure of herself.

"It was Ricky from the gelato station, wasn't it?" The staff knew everything about everyone, and Ricky had a crush on Josie, so she worked it for all it was worth.

"Ricky called him a giggle-loo. 'Likes skinny ones best, but any size okay from the penthouses,' he told me. Gave me an extra scoop of Mango Madness, too."

I didn't want to believe her, but I guess she was right. Nothing from you showed up—not a postcard, note, email—nothing.

On October 14th, I had to take my computer to the Apple Store, and the technician who was trying to unscramble a mess I had made informed me that I had two email boxes.

"What?"

"Yeah, he said. "There's the one you've been using, and another one, with 400 unread messages."

Two were from you. The first, sent two days after I left the ship, said, "I miss you already. Don't get married." The second one, sent October 11th, said, "I remember every word of our conversation and can hardly wait to get home so we can talk. I'd jump ship if we weren't in the middle of the Atlantic Ocean."

I sat on Apple's stool in a dazed euphoria and two weeks later my phone rang, and it was you.

"I'm back in Sun Valley, but I caught something awful on the plane coming home," you croaked.

"Why don't we email until you feel better?" I suggested.

"Good idea, but remember, don't get married."

I was thrilled and could hardly wait to tell Josie that you had called. I tracked her down at Frank's Gym, where we had to go three times a week because Alex said my arms were too weak to give enough resistance to a dance partner, and he told Josie she needed to strengthen her legs.

First time out, I dropped a three-pound weight on Frank's foot, and Josie flew backwards off the treadmill and knocked Frank off his feet.

Frank made workout programs for us—mine was weights, the rowing machine, and a pulley-deal, and Josie's was the Stairmaster and the Squat machine—and then he stayed far away from us. It was easy to pop in on the way to Safeway, and over the years I worked my way up to fifteen-pound curls, thirty-five pounds on the rower, and forty pounds on the pulley.

"Romeo is playing you," Josie said, huffing on the Stairmaster. "He's been around, knows what he's doing, and you are ripe for plucking."

"That's not so," I said. I picked up a ten pounder in each hand to warm up and started my curls. "He had no reason to call unless he really wants to connect with me."

"You're a romantic fool, you lost all your senses at sea, and now you're plunging overboard." Josie said. "Also, you've still got some flab hanging off your arms."

*　　　*　　　*

Right or wrong, I dove in, heart first.

Emails, notes, clippings, book exchanges; all the trappings of a mutual enchantment began, and finally, when you stopped wheezing and sneezing, the phone calls started, but there was so much to share and never enough time, and I wanted to see and touch you.

When my phone rang one Monday evening in early November, I hoped it was you. It was.

"Guess what, little Cara?" you asked.

"What?"

"I have friends in San Francisco, and they're throwing a huge black-tie anniversary party at the Hotel Nikko. Will you go with me?"

"I'd be delighted, Mr. Romano. Just give me the date."

I was sure you could hear my heart pounding. Was this actually going to happen? I longed to see you, to talk, to touch—just to be with you again.

"I'll have to call you back. I got so excited, I left the invitation in the mailbox," you said.

The date of the party was November 16 and the logistics were tricky. You were flying into San Francisco the day before and renting a car, and your friends were putting up guests at the hotel the night of the party.

"But I'd like to see you when I get in on the 15th," you said.

You had no idea how far away my little town of Clayton was, tucked in the shadow of Mt. Diablo.

"Well, Clayton is about eight miles east of Walnut Creek, and it's a long way from SFO. If you drove over here, you could stay at a Holiday Inn that's about a mile away. We could spend the afternoon and evening together and drive together to the party the next day."

"Excellent plan. I'll book everything right now. Can't wait to see you, little one."

Josie scoffed at the whole thing. "He won't show. When he figures out how long it would take to get to Clayton from SFO, he'll just go directly to the Nikko, and you just wasted big bucks on a new dress."

"He will too show, and I'm not the least bit sorry about the dress or the shoes," I said.

But what if she was right? By the morning of November 15, my mind was in a complete tizzy. Would you look the same? What if I didn't feel the overwhelming attraction anymore? What if you didn't?

I finally took half a Zanax, and when you pulled into the driveway and stepped out of the car holding a lavish bouquet of red roses, you looked every bit as dashing as I remembered. Maybe your nose was a little bigger than I recalled, but it gave you character.

We hugged and shared our very first kiss. You never were much of a kisser— maybe because your nose got in the way—but it didn't matter. I felt so safe, so protected with you.

"Boy, I sure could use a cup of coffee," you said as you stepped through the door.
Uh-oh. "I don't have any coffee. I don't even have a coffee pot. Lots of tea, though."

The rest of the day and evening dissolved into a hundred laughs. No food in the fridge except for some eggs, brie, and a decadent chocolate torte that I had spent two days fretting over.

"Let us eat cake," I said, and we were off to K-Mart for a coffee pot and to Safeway for coffee.

"I am going to stock your refrigerator with a few essentials," you insisted. Salami, roasted red peppers, capers, and of course, prosciutto went into the cart.

You couldn't hold out long enough to get back to the house for coffee, so we had a late lunch on the deck at Ed's Mudville Grill, the informal town center where everyone hung out, dogs included. You loved the western feel of everything and the closeness of Mt. Diablo. You also loved your Rueben sandwich and fries. I had forgotten how men eat.

Back at the house, we practiced a few dance steps so we could show off at the party and by then the sun had gone down.

"I think it's Happy Hour," you said. "I could sure use a scotch."

Uh-oh. "I don't have any scotch. Lot's of wine, though."

Back to Safeway for a bottle of scotch, which I insisted on buying due to my inadequate hosting, and then you bought a bottle of something called Sambuca. I had forgotten how men drink.

So, dinner consisted of cheese, crackers, prosciutto, roasted red peppers, chocolate torte, wine and scotch.

You never made it to the Holiday Inn.

After my mom died, I turned her bedroom into a little office and the other bedroom into a television and reading room. That left the master bedroom with a California king size bed or the living room sofa as sleeping options.

After a nightcap or two of Sambuca, it seemed silly for you to be scrunched up on the sofa, so, a bit tipsy, we agreed to share the big bed—but no sex. A little cuddle perhaps, but it was too soon for more.

I spent half an hour trying to make myself look seductive, and when I came out of the bathroom, you were already in bed and half asleep. You had placed a little piece of wrapped chocolate on my pillow, just as they did on the ship—so endearing.

"Come here, my little Cara," you mumbled and pulled me close to you. You felt and smelled so wonderfully masculine. I snuggled in, spoon style, and I could feel your breath on my neck. Heaven!

Then you started to snore, right into my ear. Your arm was around me and felt like it weighed 30 of your 185 pounds. You were a petrified log, and I couldn't wake you or move. Hour after hour I lay entrapped. At times, the bed shook as if a 5.0 earthquake was rolling underneath.

God, with no sleep, how was I going to be charming tomorrow? It was well into tomorrow, about 4 a.m., when you finally rolled over and I could move and muffle the sound a little with my pillow. Maybe you weren't so popular in the penthouses after all.

You woke up about 8:30, quite refreshed. I no longer cared about being seductive—the need for sleep and survival were paramount.

"Buon giorno, my little Cara. Did you sleep well?"

"Nick, do you know you snore—big time?" I rasped.

"Was it that bad? Sometimes when I had to share a room with other hosts, they would go bunk with the waiters."

"Well, Josie snores, too, and she bought strips at the drug store to put on her nose."

"You go back to sleep, and I'll go to the drug store. When I get back, we can have some breakfast."

I woke up at about 10:30 to the smell of coffee and bacon. You had made scrambled eggs, hash browns, and toast with marmalade—a feast. And on the kitchen counter were a container of nose drops and a box of nose strips.

"The pharmacist thought the nose strips might not be big enough. They only come in one size, so he suggested the drops as a backup."

I thought your nose was distinguished, no matter how much noise it made. After I did the dishes, we had a lovely day, sitting on the deck, you with your coffee, me with my tea, taking in the view of Mt. Diablo.

The rains would not come for a few weeks, so the grassy knolls on the mountain were still burnt umber from the summer's sun, and the air had that soft sweetness that usually began in September.

We talked. I loved your stories about your family and growing up in an environment wildly different from mine. Your mother raised five kids without much help from a husband with an eye for the ladies.

"I left for school one morning and Mom tucked a note in the breast pocket of my jacket. We had to wear trousers, white shirts with ties, and preppy jackets, and all the St. John's kids learned to run like hell to and from school so we wouldn't be smacked around by the street punks.

"Anyway, she told me to read the note after school and do what it said. When I read it, she said that we didn't live over the pool hall anymore and to go to the address in the note. She had found a little garret apartment a few blocks away and moved out everything.

"My dad was livid, publically humiliated because Mom had enlisted the neighbors to help her move while he was at work. It didn't take him long to find us.

"What's the matter with you, woman? He hollered at the garret window from the street and I was embarrassed, but Mom wouldn't let him in. Turns out he had moved one of his mistresses into an apartment across from the pool hall. That was the last straw for Mom."

"How did she support you?"

"Well, by that time, my eldest brother, Mike, had run away because the loan sharks were after him. The next oldest joined the army, and my sister snagged the first guy she could find who had a job, got married and split as fast as she could. That left Harry, who was a couple of years older, and me. Mom worked at home, sewing sequins and lace on fancy gowns for Saks.

"My mom worked for ten years to pay back what Mike owed the bookie. Took a lot of sequins on a lot of dresses. Mike was a real schmuck.

"Anyway, Harry and I worked for my best friend's father after school. He had a warehouse and needed us strong kids to move stuff in and out. Mr. Bruno stood by as we loaded and unloaded the trucks and took inventory on his clipboard. He cautioned us every day. 'Boys,' he said, 'trusta nobody.' Best advice I ever got."

"Wow. We were raised on different planets," I said.

"I think you were a rich, lovely princess and probably spoiled rotten."

"Hardly. My mom was seventeen and Dad was twenty-one when they met at a dance. She was pretty and a flirt and could do the best Charleston in town. Dad looked a lot like Ronald Reagan and wowed her with a Continental because only Fred Astaire could dance it in the movies. They eloped two weeks later.

"Four years later, I showed up. They had about given up on a baby, when Mom went to a new doctor, and he told her to stand on her head right after the deed. She was agile, and it worked."

"I was teasing before, but I bet your folks really did spoil you."

"Yes and no. Mom wanted to raise a perfect child since she couldn't have more kids. She protected me from all possible harm. Scrubbed the house, floor to ceiling, doused me in baby-bubbles three times a day, and fed me until I was a butterball. Mom recorded every burble, crawl, step and word in my baby book, but then the pages went blank."

"Why?"

"Because the unthinkable happened. Polio. I don't remember much except I was placed in the big bedroom, my grandmother's wringer washing machine was rolled in, and the grownups took shifts spending day and night applying hot compresses to my body."

"Jesus!"

"That was just the beginning, but you'll have to wait for the rest of the story because we've got to get dressed or we'll be late for the party."

"It's only 4:00."

"We'll be two hours getting through the tunnel on a Saturday night. Are you hungry?" I asked.

"No. I finished off the cheese and prosciutto while we were talking."

We went upstairs, and I put on my new black beaded gown and my new shoes that only hurt a little bit. I heard what I thought was a curse coming from the office, which had been designated as your dressing room.

"Marone! Goddamned harness. I need some help in here," you called out. I was getting used to Italian curse words sprinkled about. They sounded kind of cute.

I had never assisted a man in putting on formal wear, but by the time I plunged my hands into your waistband and got all those little buttons on your suspenders affixed to the interior of your pants, I felt we had been more intimate than if we had made love. The tie was another challenge, needing to be woven through loops under your stiff shirt collar.

When you were all together, you adjusted your pocket hankie, stood back, and asked, "How do I look?"

"Splendid," I said, suppressing thoughts of what I now knew to be inside your trousers. "But how did you manage to get dressed on the ship?"

"The hosts help one another out. You look gorgeous. Andiamo! I want to hear the rest of your story."

We buckled up in the rental car, and I picked up where I had left off.

"I was terrified, and all these people kept shaking their heads and saying, 'What a pity. She was so cute,' as if I wasn't there anymore.

"Finally, I was moved back into my room and into my junior bed, but I couldn't walk. My right foot flopped down and wouldn't come up.

"Next, they put an iron brace on my leg that weighed more than me. I had a home teacher because nobody knew if I was still contagious, and I couldn't drag around that brace anyway. From the age of five until I was eight, I was trapped in that awful thing. Finally, my parents saved enough money to have a surgeon operate. If I tell you the procedure, you probably won't want dinner."

"That could never happen."

"Well, at that time, the only remedy for a dropped foot was to cut the Achilles tendon, move it and some other stuff around, and use other muscles to pull up the foot. It was horrible, but when the casts were finally off, I could walk, because my foot was flat.

"But now it wouldn't go down, I couldn't point my toes, and my leg started to twist. So that demon in a white coat operated again and fused the bones in my ankle. Now my foot wouldn't go up or down. Then, because my right leg was shorter than the left, Dr. Sawbones proposed to cut down my left leg to the same length.

"Mom usually deferred to white coats, but not this time. We were sitting together in the torturer's examining room, and I clutched her hand, petrified."

'What? You want to amputate my daughter's good leg and then reattach it?' She shrieked.

'Well, in a manner of speaking. It's a new procedure, and Cara might have back problems in her later years if we don't try it out.'

"Mom stood up, dragged me to the door, walked out, and slammed the door so hard that we heard one of his diplomas fall off the wall. That's the last time I ever went anywhere near an orthopedist."

"You know what?" you asked.

"What?"

"You deserve to be a princess, and I want to spoil you rotten."

*　　　*　　　*

The party was elegant. Champagne fountains, a chocolate waterfall, a live band, and a huge dance floor that we played on all evening, with no Hungarians to dodge. The host and hostess were lovely, graciously introducing us to others, and made me feel super welcome. When the party ended, we went to bed with the same rules in effect, and you plastered your nose with white strips, which helped quell both the noise and my ardor.

The next day, we gobbled up all we could of San Francisco: Golden Gate Park, the De Young Museum, Fisherman's Wharf, and we ended up in North Beach eating the best spaghettini I'd ever tasted.

"Let's go home," you said, and when we arrived in Clayton, you opened the car door for me, ushered me into the house, and said, "I want this to be my home, too."

"You mean Clayton?"

"No, I mean here, right here with you. Let me stay the week, and if it works, I'll sell my place and come here."

"What about your life there? Your friends, your condo, and all your things?"

"I have too much stuff, and I'll sell it along with my condo. The only thing I'd bring is my breadbox. And we can always go visit my friends."

Were you insane? Not any more so than I. The protocol in the bedroom changed, and we couldn't get enough of each other. I guess you got a lot of practice in those penthouses, because you were an incredible lover. At the end of the week, I made one stipulation—no more hosting.

"Not a problem. I was sick of having to pander to all those biddies. I just want a quiet life with you, little one. You are the most gentle, kind, and loving woman I have ever known, and I think you will be spoiling me more than I will be spoiling you."

You left to disengage yourself from Sun Valley,

and when I brought Josie up to date, she blew every gasket.

"Insane! You don't know anything about him, and he's going to take you for a ride for your money."

"He doesn't know I have any and anyway it's all locked up in a trust."

I had saved carefully over those 33 years of labor, and at one point I scraped together every dollar I had to make a one-time, ten-year investment paying 8% interest. Then I got a bundle from a deceased bachelor great-uncle who felt sorry for me as a kid, and I inherited Mom's savings and her simple little house. She and my dad had bought it for $600 in 1937, and I sold it for $250,000. So, to my bemusement, my town house on the golf course was paid for, as was my Camry, and I still had close to a million bucks.

"Besides, Nick's had a crack at women who have multi-millions, so why would he even bother with me, if money was his motive. I think he's in love with me as much as I am with him," I said.

"If your mother were still alive, she'd knock some sense into you."

"Well, she ran off with my dad two weeks after

they met, and they were happy until he died 55 years later."

"Dreamer. Shifty is shifty, and I know what I'm looking at—remember, we Chinese are shrewd, and you are a starry-eyed, gullible gringo."

*   *   *

I guess I was, but I didn't care. I was totally besotted and never doubted for a moment that this huge life-change could bring anything but happiness.

For two months, multiple phone calls kept me up to date. A ski buddy bought your condo, and then you had a giant estate sale.

"I must not have very good taste, because there was a lot left over that I had to donate. Imagine, no one wanted my Norse headboard. Do you have much extra closet space?" You asked.

"Tons. There's nothing in the closets in either the T.V. or office rooms and they're big. Plus, you can have the other upstairs bathroom all to yourself."

"Well then, I'm on my way, sweet Cara. Put some food in the frig and make room for my breadbox. Should be there in three days."

The anticipation was almost unbearable. I had already stocked the refrigerator and made a nice little space on the kitchen counter for your breadbox.

When you finally pulled into the driveway, you had a U-Haul attached to your Camero, and there was a large object filling the back seat that looked to be about two and a half feet by three feet.

Uh-oh.

"For you, my love," you said as you stepped out of the car and handed me a lovely bouquet of white and yellow roses. Then you hugged me tightly, gave me the biggest kiss possible, considering the size of your nose, and I knew it would somehow work out.

The thing in the back seat was your breadbox, and you were so proud of it.

"Genuine replica of an 18th century French breadbox," you said, and you carefully lifted it out of the car and placed it on the driveway.

It had turrets and feet, and a small door, and it was dark and huge. I could imagine Quasimoto poking a misshaped hand through the door to snatch a baguette.

"What's in the U-Haul?" I asked, trying to mask my trepidation.

"Just a few essentials," you said. "Let me show you and then I need a cup of coffee."

The U-Haul held two bicycles, skis, snowshoes, hiking poles, four boxes of shoes, three wardrobe containers stuffed with clothes, a box filled with bottles of liquor, and more boxes filled with books.

I needed a Zanax.

Somehow, you got all that stuff stored either in the house or garage. "I learned how to organize things when I worked for Mr. Bruno at the warehouse. 'Trusta nobody,' he always said, and he was right."

The only thing that didn't work out to your liking was the fact that there was absolutely nowhere to hang the breadbox unless we put it in a bathroom.

"Look, there's space in the kitchen if we put it on the floor."

"No, it has to be hung," you insisted, and I detected a glimmer of stubbornness and a touch of belligerence.

"But it has feet and looks really nice under the window," I said.

"Whatever," you said, but you were not happy about it. Our first little dust-up, but I couldn't produce an extra wall.

*   *   *

So, our new lives began.

We were invited out to many dinners and social functions by my friends, who were convinced that I had either had a stroke or seizure of some sort to behave so rashly.

Your friends and family were equally astonished, and we finally took a grand tour to New York, Maine, Connecticut, Florida, Pennsylvania, Georgia, and Idaho so they could see for themselves that you did not require a conservator.

I was scrutinized by your brothers, sister, son, daughter, all of their spouses, three grandchildren, ski and golf buddies, and assorted friends scattered from state to state, each of whom courteously and impolitely grilled me on politics, religion, ethnicity, NFL team preferences, and my views on the troubled situation between Israel and Palestine.

By the time that trip was over, I needed a conservator and a refill on my Zanax.

We got on with the business of living together. You joined the golf club, and I played bridge, went to the gym to terrorize Frank, had my dance lessons with Alex, and tried to resurrect my skills in the kitchen. Your hearing was fading, and I could hear the grass grow, so we compromised with TV ears for you until you finally caved and got hearing aids.

I learned to live with coffee, the smell of which I detested, but you were addicted, and soon new devices appeared in the kitchen—a grinder, a French press, and smelly machines for espresso and cappuccino.

"It's nice the way you keep the house so freshly aired," you commented. *Yes, wasn't it?* Oh well, annoyances faded with cuddles and kisses, and vanished completely in the bedroom.

We went to Alex's group dance classes, and he turned us on to three private ballroom dance clubs, where we made new friends who dazzled us with their quicksteps and Pasa Doblas.

A fellow named Marcello gave weekly Argentine Tango lessons not too far away, so we joined his class. I bought a fringed blouse that I thought would be fun to wear to Marcello's, but it was tricky to get into, and I was five minutes behind schedule when I ran downstairs to jump in the car to go to a lesson. I stopped mid-way, startled.

You were standing at the bottom of the stairs, red-faced with fury.

"I can't stand lateness," you yelled. You went on and on about how terrible I was for this transgression, and by the time you finished your tirade, I felt deflated and worthless, and all the joy had been stomped out of the evening. I had never experienced such anger directed at me, but I was afraid to say anything for fear you would lash out again.

Marcello announced his annual tango tour for his students to Buenos Aires, and you were the first to say, "Let's go," as if nothing had happened. I was still hurting so much that I stepped all over Marcello's feet. Yours, too.

We went. For two weeks, the group had lessons in the afternoon, and Marcello escorted us to parties, called milongas, in the evening that were held in grand dance halls built in the thirties, with iron cages for elevators and thirty-foot ceilings, and iron balconies on which one could imagine Eva Peron holding forth.

Around 10 p.m. the tango masters would appear, usually men in their 50's or 60's with incredibly sensual middle-aged women. Resounding applause welcomed them, and then they would take our breaths away with their intense, erotic performances.

The city felt so European, with small cafés and restaurants on every corner serving every imaginable cuisine and wines to match. We went to the pampas and watched the gauchos on horseback thunder down racetracks with poles, competing to spear overhanging rings.

You were your usual, exuberant self, smuggling a bottle of homemade Limoncello all the way back to California. But the pain from your dressing down months before was still with me, as was the fear that more might come.

This was the era of timeshares. Offers to stay in fancy resorts poured in, and all we had to do was sit and listen to a spiel for 90 minutes, and then we were free to play at the resort, usually with a gift of one or two hundred dollars for spending money.

Our first adventure was to Park City, Utah, where we watched ski jumpers practicing on slide runs built for the Olympics, soaring in the air, twisting and turning, and then landing in pools of water.

At Hilton Head, South Carolina, we went for a walk in a park along a stream and stared in astonishment at alligators lounging on people's lawns and porches. It was a short walk.

In Sedona, we succumbed to the red rock of Arizona—the Bell, the Cathedral, the Chimney— the entire region was spectacular, and we bought a timeshare and went back time and again. On one trip, we went to all fourteen vortexes, not once having a revelation.

Often, we drove down the California coast, sometimes to Pacifica for clam chowder at Sam's, or farther down to Carmel, Monterey, Pismo Beach, or Santa Barbara.

Once, on the way to Pismo beach, we saw a cluster of cars and stopped to see what was going. We had stumbled upon Elephant Seal Beach at exactly the right time. Every year, the seals return to give birth and hundreds of the enormous beasts covered the beach. Females were either giving birth or tending to their newborn pups, while the males bellowed and reared up to fight in the water. An amazing sight.

More timeshares—Charleston, Savannah, San Antonio, Chicago—I no longer remember the order.

Then we discovered Santa Fe. Desert, I thought, packing lightweight clothing, but it was high desert, at about seven thousand feet. I froze and I loved it.

The vista's, the pueblos, the explosions of color and creativity were overwhelming. Even the freeway overpasses were painted in motifs celebrating the tribes of the area.

We drank ourselves into stupors at Maria's Bar and Restaurant—over 100 variations of Margaritas, every one a gem—and put in a reservation to eat at the Shed, where two day's notice was required because of the superb food. It was there that we learned to specify New Mexican when ordering. Special blends of green and red chilies and blue corn turned the most common of dishes into gourmet fare.

Canyon Road was a revelation. Artists, sculptors, galleries—days worth of art to explore plus the Georgia O'Keeffe museum down the next street. And New Mexican food was everywhere, and absolutely delicious. I feared I might become an eighteen-wheeler.

Taos, an ancient pueblo, was only about an hour away and if we took the upper road, we could stop at Rancho De Chimayo, a landmark restaurant, for a feast. Then onward, over the bridge that spanned the Rio Grande Gorge. It was narrow, only two lanes, but cement walkways led to a few outcroppings for taking in the gorge and the 600-foot drop to the river.

You exchanged the Sedona timeshare, because there was no question.

Santa Fe was our place.

*   *   *

You put in a lot of time planning all these trips, which required much research on the computer, and you hated the computer, but you did not trust travel agents to secure reservations.

Sometimes your frustration would boil over into shouting matches and you would curse and rage at automated voices—and sometimes real people were on the other end of the line, and I felt embarrassed and sorry for them, but I said nothing because I didn't want you to turn your anger toward me. I wondered if all Italians had such explosive tempers.

Once, I was in the kitchen and I heard cursing, a loud thump, and then there was total silence. I was afraid you might have fallen, so I went upstairs to the office. You were sitting, stone-faced and still at the computer and the Interval book you used for looking up timeshare information had been ripped apart and thrown on the floor.

"What happened?" I dared to ask.

"Well," you said in a calm, dulcet tone, "I was completing a renewal form for the timeshare and it took forever. I kept typing in the information on the computer and finally got to the end, where it asked for a signature. I picked up my pen and signed it— on the computer screen. I'm going for a walk now, before I have a heart attack."

You got up and left, thank God, because I couldn't keep from laughing. I found the screen cleaner, and most of the ink came off, but "Dominic Romano" was forever etched on that screen, and you stubbornly refused to get another computer until that one died three years later.

*   *   *

Josie had no interest in our domestic travels. We asked her along many times, but she declined, saying that we needed time to ourselves. The real reason was that she was still convinced you were a smarmy gold-digger.

I always thought her suspicious nature stemmed from the painful betrayal in her childhood. She was the first-born of parents still rooted deeply in traditional Chinese culture, and she was doted upon until a baby brother arrived when she was eight years old.

"Man, did they ever shut me out. I was toast and my brother Johnny was emperor of the household. I got even whenever I could. Once, my father came home with a bright red wagon that I had seen at the hardware store.

"I got real excited, but my dad said it was for Johnny, not me. So, I got a can of white paint out of the garage, climbed up on the roof, and sure enough, that dumb little cluck parked the wagon right where I wanted it. I took care of his red wagon. Got some of the paint on him, too, but it was worth the two months detention and no allowance."

Dismissing our offers, she instead pursued Jon's itinerary, but when she got back from New Zealand on a repositioning cruise, she caught a bad flu.

"Fuck! Goddamned gambu again. I should sue United for their crappy hand sanitizers," she sniffled. But then the sneezes turned to a bad cough, and I took her to John Muir Emergency, and the cough turned into bronchitis, then to acute bronchitis with a touch of pneumonia.

She was wiped out for a month, and you were

wonderful—driving her to doctors' appointments when I couldn't, making pizzas and spaghetti for her and delivering the food to her door.

"I can't believe it," you said after a delivery of meatballs. "She actually let me in her house, all the way to the kitchen."

"You mean she's never asked you in before?" I asked.

"I think she's like Mr. Bruno—trusta nobody," you said. Well, she certainly didn't trust you.

*   *   *

Somewhere along the line, about two years in, we decided to get married. You had already bought me an outrageously expensive engagement ring—a brilliant oval-cut diamond that I loved.

"Insurance. I don't want any other guy to think you're available," you said.

A brochure from Star Sapphire started the discussion. The Norwegian Fjords were featured, and you insisted that I had to see them, even though you'd been on four cruises that went there already.

"Wouldn't it be fun to be married aboard ship?" I said, half in jest. The idea was so foolishly romantic and appealing to us both that I booked the cruise.

You wanted to pay for it, but that didn't seem right because I had so much more money than you. Our pensions were about the same, but as near as I could tell, you had about $100,000 socked away or probably less after the ring. You were very secretive about your business, be it financial or whatever. You guarded your computer as if it held the treasures of the Uffizi.

I wondered what information required that level of protection, but every time I looked at the screen etched with your name, I got the giggles and let it go.

Josie and I arranged our private dance lessons with Alex so we could have a late lunch of tacos and iced tea at the Guadalajara on Tuesdays. I had to let her know what we were planning because there were financial consequences that would affect her.

Years before, we made a pact. We were both childless, I had no family, and she hated her brother, so we drew up trusts leaving each other all assets if one of us bit the dust.

I couldn't stand the thought of my beloved

without a roof over his head while coping with my demise, so this is what I proposed to Josie.

"What if I amend my trust, giving him life estate in the house?"

"This means you would own the property, but he could live there, paying modest expenses like the Homeowners Association dues, until he croaked. He'd have to live there and could not rent out the property or bring anyone else in. If he moved, he'd be out."

Josie thought a long time and asked for a refill on her iced tea. Then she squinted, a shrewd look crept over her face, and she smiled a Cheshire smile.

"I know I can't talk you out of marrying that ass and I don't give a shit how much spaghetti he brings me, but if we do what you're suggesting, I could end up being lover-boy's landlady. He wouldn't last two months with me at the helm. It's a deal."

So I amended my trust, you and I agreed to split the cost of the cruise, and then we found out that the Captain would renew vows, but not perform marriages.

On the Friday before the Saturday sailing, we

took Josie with us to the Court House to be our witness, stood in line with half a dozen pregnant teenagers, and were married.

"Lover-boy's landlord. Imagine the possibilities," Josie whispered to me as the clerk in a tee shirt threw on a judge's black robe and ushered us into a little room to conduct the ceremony and sign the papers. I decided I had better live a long life.

*   *   *

What a honeymoon. The Sapphire felt like home, and the first stop was Copenhagen. I'd never seen the sea of bicyclists, men and women dressed for business in formal suits, who weaved through the busy streets and squares.

Norway was everything you said it would be. The Geiragen Fjord with it's Seven Sisters Falls roaring down the mountainside, and opposite, across the fjord, Friaren, said to be flirting with the Sisters, thundering with equal ferocity. Mile after nautical mile of hundreds of mesmerizing falls.

Nor had I been to Stockholm, where the waterways and architecture were entrancing, and we ate Swedish meatballs for breakfast, lunch, and dinner.

On the flight back, I think you left your libido with United Airlines, because you went from loving groom to indifferent grouch within 24 hours of our arrival back in Clayton. What had happened? I was still full of moonbeams and meatballs, and you seemed full of bile.

I was in the kitchen making a vegetable soup that you liked and had just squeezed the garlic in a press. I flipped it open to clean out the detritus when you came up behind me.

I thought you were going to put your arms around me, maybe kiss the back of my neck, and nibble my ear.

No. You stood very close, still behind me, and screamed in my ear.

"You are a terrible, wasteful person. Look at you, throwing out perfectly good food. And I want dinner on the table at five every day."

"But you don't get home from playing golf until seven," I said, bewildered and shocked.

"Always an argument, and always your way," you roared, your face purple with rage. You went upstairs, slammed the door to the T.V. room, stormed by me when you went to the kitchen for food, ate alone behind the closed door in the T.V.

room, or went out to eat by yourself, slept on the couch, and didn't speak to me for three days. I was stunned.

And then the storm was over. You came home from golf, became your usual, affectionate self, and acted as if nothing had happened. I was a wreck.

About three weeks later, we were driving to Napa to have lunch at Don Giovanni's, your favorite restaurant in the valley. I had the MapQuest directions in hand, and you had taken out a regular map even though we'd been there half a dozen times. You asked what came next, and I hesitated slightly.

You pulled over to the side of the road, slammed on the brakes, and screamed at me, "Can't you even read a simple map?" You snatched the MapQuest paper from my hands, tore it up and crumpled up the regular map and threw them in the back seat.

Your face was purple, and I was terrified. You made an illegal U turn, drove in silent fury all the way home, and once again withdrew to the T.V. room for three days, going about your usual day quite normally, but treating me as if I were the enemy.

What was wrong? I was too afraid to talk to you, so I left a note for you on the kitchen table.

"What has happened to the wonderful, loving man I just married? I don't understand what is going on, but I want that man back."

I disappeared for the day, afraid of how you would react to the note, but when I came home, you had written on the bottom of the note, "Me too."

When you came in from golf, you sat down on a kitchen chair and told me about some pills you had been taking for years for depression, but you stopped taking them when we decided to get married.

"Why?" I asked.

"Because they were for depression, and I wasn't depressed. I was very happy."

"So you've been off the pills for a couple of months?"

"That's about right."

"I think you need them, because the man I married is still missing."

You renewed your prescription, promised to take the pills, and within a couple of weeks, you were back to normal. We called them your happy pills, and you were supposed to take one in the morning and one in the late afternoon, but you didn't always remember to take the second one, and I could tell right away. Your thought pattern would change, and you would become negative and suspicious.

Why hadn't you told me about the medication— pride, embarrassment, shame? I didn't know, but I did know that I needed help.

I found a therapist who figured out what was going on in about ten minutes. I spent the first three sessions crying my heart out.

I loved you so much, and you put up a terrible wall of anger and rejection, and I despaired, and then you would tear the wall down and overwhelm me with love and affection. I never knew who was coming through the door, the you I loved or this raging stranger who appeared every three or four weeks.

"I can't diagnose someone I've never met, but these mood swings sound excessive, and usually a person with this type of disorder will be helped by a mood stabilizer more than by an anti-depressant," my therapist said. "His mood swings will cycle, even with the pills, but they shouldn't be as extreme as you describe."

She gave me the name of a shrink who specialized in this type of mood disorder, and with great trepidation, I passed the information on to you. To my surprise, you said you would make an appointment. I called you afterward to see how things went, and you said, "She's wonderful. We're meeting again next week."

I was so relieved, so happy that you would be getting help, so hopeful.

Of course, I am now familiar with your tone of voice when you are lying, and there was no follow-up appointment if there ever was a first.

*   *   *

So when it was good, it was very good. You heard me say that I had always wanted to go inside the Colosseum and Forum in Rome and to go to Pompeii but had not because the tour book said that the walking was too hazardous.

"Those tour guides are full of crap. You could easily walk either. Let's go."

I booked us on the Sapphire, and we again sailed the Mediterranean. I walked through the Forum, hand-in-hand with you, and I stood inside the Colosseum. I could hear my Latin teacher expounding on the glories of ancient Rome, and the expectations she held for her students. The honor of a Latin student was above reproach, and the high road was always to be taken. I always tried.

Pompeii was even more compelling than I had imagined, and Herculaneum an unexpected treasure. It was a thrill to be there, and I would never have experienced any of it without your support. You were wonderful the whole trip—kind, funny, loving, attentive—a second honeymoon with the real you, and I was in love again.

Lots more travel—Zion, Bryce, three corners of the Grand Canyon, back to Santa Fe, a cruise to Australia where we played in a park full of wallabies and ended up in Singapore at the zoo in a minor monsoon, and I got to hold a baby gorilla on my lap. Onward to Belgium, because you wanted to eat mussels in Brussels.

Some airports were so huge that the airlines provided carts to get to the right terminals, and we found out that I could ask for wheelchair assistance when there were no carts. You loved it because we were then allowed to board first, and I was relieved because a fast-paced two-mile trek to a boarding gate was exhausting.

Next, you wanted to see the beaches in Normandy, and I wanted to see the countryside and villages. We flew to Paris—lots more honeymoon—and then rented a car, but you forgot to specify one with a navigation system.

"Won't matter," you said. "I'm still pretty fluent in French, and I've got half a dozen maps. Thank God I couldn't read French so I couldn't be held responsible. We wound this way and that, hour after hour, and I swear we drove through Chartre three times before you stopped to ask for help at a restaurant.

"It's seven o'clock. Might as well eat here," you said, and you engaged the fellow who had opened the door for you in what appeared to be a disjointed and somewhat argumentative discussion.

Finally, an impossibly svelte woman intervened, shrugging her shoulders in that dismissive way that only the French can pull off, and we were seated. It was a long wait for dinner, because the restaurant did not open until 8:30. Your French wasn't so hot after all.

That clever woman could sense your ugly American storm coming, and our table was quickly graced with a basket of warm breads, cheeses, and a bottle of wine with which to kill time. A second bottle was required to complement the superb meal, served at exactly 8:30, and a spot of port accompanied the crème brûlée. I think there was some brandy, too. We staggered to the inn next door and spent the night because we couldn't find our way back to the car, let alone to the timeshare.

Our hangovers were massive, but you drank half a bottle of Campari, persevered, and we found the beaches the next day. The road followed the curves of the beaches but was high enough so that the sea and entire beachfront could be seen.

Waves rolled up from the sea and onto the beige sand beaches. Long green grasses grew wild up the hillside to where the memorials were protectively shrouded by many trees. The quiet was overpowering, and an enveloping sense of peace belied the carnage that had unfolded that fateful day in 1944.

We moved silently from section to section. There were five, each named for and designated to honor the men who had exited from their ships, fought through the waters, hit their beach, and died, along with their comrades who had been blown from the sky. Utah and Omaha were for the Americans, Gold and Sword for the British, Juno for the Canadians. The designs of each memorial were varied—rolling lawns, acres of crosses, stone monuments—but all were humbling, and we sat on a bench near Omaha and cried until the emotions for many wars and many deaths were spent.

*   *   *

And then it went bad, and it was horrid.

"Let's do this cruise that starts in Japan and ends in China," you suggested, and it sounded fine to me. Two tours were available when we docked in Japan, either Tokyo or Hiroshima, and we chose the latter because neither of us had been there. It was a wise decision.

The Peace Memorial in Hiroshima was stunning. Only one structure, the Genbaku Dome, had survived the atomic bomb, a stark ruin left as a reminder to all of the devastations of war. The park itself was elegant in its simplicity. Reflecting pools, statuary, monuments, and a museum filled with pictures, artifacts, and two riveting models of the city, before and after the bomb, that graphically defined horror and hope.

I don't recall much else because I could detect a change in you as we boarded for China.

You were distant on the ship, way out of sorts when we disembarked in Beijing, took no interest in the astounding building frenzy to accommodate the pending Olympics, or the pollution that turned the sky to mud, or the fun, if obligatory, rickshaw ride into old Beijing.

I was impressed with the elegance of the hotel where we were spending the night, and apprehensive because of your sour countenance. Most hotel guests were Asian, and when we entered the crystal infused restaurant for dinner, we were the only Caucasians.

The room was hushed as diners quietly went about consuming outrageously priced delicacies such as shark fin soup and abalone. You sat across the table, glowering, and after we were served, you ate about two bites of food, stood up, threw your napkin at me, yelled, "This is such shit," and stormed out of the dining room. All chopsticks ceased clicking, and all Asian eyes were downcast, averted to spare me more embarrassment.

I sat there, completely humiliated and terrified of going to our room. A hostess came over and asked if she could be of assistance, and I thanked her and said, "No, please just charge everything to our room bill."

She kindly took my hand and walked with me through the whispers filling the room. "We have other rooms available if you need one," she murmured discretely as I stepped into the elevator.

I could feel your fury through the door as I approached, and once in the room, you snarled that you wanted nothing to do with me and that you didn't want to talk or deal with my sniveling.

From the hotel to the airport to two connecting flights to the sedan transport to Clayton, you never spoke one word to me. Thirty-six hours of hostile silence.

And when we arrived home, you continued to behave as if I didn't exist, and when you resumed talking to me, the word "Please" disappeared from your vocabulary. Orders. Stark orders and pronouncements.

"Cancel the trip to Istanbul. I'm not going out of the country anymore. Not going anywhere except maybe Santa Fe. And cross off the dance clubs. I quit. I also joined a hiking club. Too bad you can't come along. Why don't you get a cane? Better yet, why don't you get one of those motorized scooter things?"

Who were you?

You systematically stripped our lives and my self-esteem to shreds. Now I was a cripple, worthy only of supplying your newfound hiking cronies with cookies. "Not that store-bought junk—make them from scratch," you demanded, and I was too afraid not to follow orders.

You presented me with a cane, the folding kind that could be carried in a handbag and admonished me for not using it.

"But I don't need it as long as I walk on flat sidewalks," I tried to explain. You unfurled that cane every time we went out the door, and it was always placed in the car whenever we went somewhere.

On one occasion, a hike was to end at a trailhead near Clayton. You again volunteered me to make cookies, so this time, instead of bringing the refreshments with you, I was to bring them and ice chests with water and beverages to meet you all at the trailhead.

I made the cookies the night before, and you packed the rest of the stuff in my car. You called me to come over to the parking area at the trailhead about 11:00.

As I drove up to the parking area, a grubby group of about twenty hikers were standing around, and they immediately came over to unload the car.

Introductions were made and everyone stood in a circle, munching, drinking, and sweating. The group leader, who clearly was in command of more than this little excursion, walked over to you and said, "So, at last we get to meet your lovely wife. Is she as cosmopolitan and erudite as you?"

You stood there, in front of all those people, shook your head indicating "no," and extended your hand, making a thumbs-down gesture.

The hurt and humiliation I felt was unbearable. I stood there, in disbelief, and some kind woman finally broke the horrified silence by saying how delicious the goddamned cookies were. Something inside me had been crushed beyond repair.

*   *   *

I scarcely spoke to you for two weeks, but you were so full of yourself, you didn't notice. You were going to Peru with the hikers and didn't even give me a hug or kiss when you left. "Arrivederci," you called out as an afterthought as you pulled out of the driveway.

When you returned two weeks later, you immersed yourself in planning many hikes, all of which required multiple pre-hikes of several days. Did I mind when you took off for Carmel, Big Sur, Monterey, Crater Lake, Ashland?

Of course not. Why should a disabled old-ish

woman hold you back when you could find multiple audiences to entice with stories of your exploits?

Once, Josie went out with her walking group, and when we met up later at the gym, she insisted she saw you at the far end of the park holding hands with a tall redheaded woman.

"Couldn't possibly have been him. He's on a pre-hike at Crater Lake," I said, but the walls of denial had begun to crack, and doubt was seeping through.

"He's a two-timing shit. Wake up, you ninny," she said.

Another friend called to chat and mentioned she had seen you having lunch at Postino, that charming restaurant in Lafayette. "At least I think it was him. He was very cozy with a brunette woman, and I waved hello, but he pretended not to see me."

"Must have been some sort of mistake, Joan. He's pre-hiking somewhere near Tahoe."

"I was three feet away," Joan said.

When you were home, you spent most of your time in the office with the door closed, engaged with either the computer or phone. I was astounded when you emerged one afternoon, nuzzled my neck, and said "How about Santa Fe? I just booked us for four nights at the timeshare."

I was thrilled. I hugged you and held you tight. Surely you could not be sneaking around, betraying me, betraying us. I was so happy and excited. This would be our first trip together in over a year, maybe two.

"I'll run over to the market and buy us the best fillets the butcher has. This is an occasion," I said.

"Don't forget my mushrooms," you added, and went back into the office and shut the door.

I didn't bother to close the garage door, since I would only be gone twenty minutes at most, and it needed an airing because that's where you stored six of the eight coffee makers you had acquired.

When I came back from the store, you had no idea I was home because you were not wearing your hearing aids. They were a nuisance when you were on the phone, and you discovered that if you turned on the speakerphone, you could get along without them.

However, you couldn't hear anything else, and you unknowingly spoke much louder without them. You forgot one thing. I could still hear the grass grow.

You were on the phone when I came in the door from the garage, and I could hear every word you said.

"Don't sweat it, hon. I know exactly how to handle her. I ignore her, treat her like she doesn't exist, order her around, and she gets all upset. Then I toss her a crumb, and she melts like butter. I'll have my name on that trust as soon as I get back from Santa Fe."

I backed out the door, got in my car, and drove to an isolated spot off Marsh Creek Road. I pulled over, stopped, and started to cry. I sobbed until my ribs hurt and no more tears could come. Next a great stillness overcame me, and then, quite literally, I saw red. Rage red, and I knew exactly what to do.

*   *   *

I returned to the house, brought in the steaks, and babbled like a bride.

"Four days at the timeshare? That is so wonderful. Maybe we'll have time to backtrack and take that tram outside Albuquerque and go to all the galleries and to Taos. You have no idea what this trip means to me." I kissed your cheek, cooked the steaks and mushrooms, opened a very fine bottle of Cabernet, and packed frothy underthings and flirty nighties.

"I put your cane in your carry-on and ordered wheelchair service from Southwest," you announced as we closed up the house.

"Whatever would I do without you," I responded, and you gave me an enormous bear hug, the likes of which I had not felt since I became such burdensome baggage.

The aura was one of celebration, and we even bought two of those little bottles of wine to drink on the flight. The plane was right on time, the rental car was ready, and we arrived at the tram site in time to catch the last car going up for the day. The view was staggering, and the sun went down to show off all the lights of the valley. No need to backtrack.

By the time we got to Santa Fe and checked in at the timeshare, it was Happy Hour at Maria's. Two house Margaritas for you, two Merry Margaritas for me, and a shared platter of rice, beans and tacos finished us off. When we collapsed into bed, you snuggled up like a loving, happy drunk. I slipped aside as soon as I knew you were asleep.

Phase one of your plan was going well. Butter her up.

"Hon," you asked the next morning, "what's on the agenda for today?"

You rotten shit. How many "hons" were out there?

"Well, sweetie, (*I, too, could lie with butter*) how about doing the galleries and museum today, and going to Taos tomorrow. We could have lunch at Chimayo on the way."

You could not have been more accommodating. We visited the dancing elephants at the Ventana Gallery, you bought me a little turquoise pendant and a pair of hand-tooled boots for yourself, and since we couldn't get into the Shed, our favorite restaurant, we ended up back at Maria's. I made sure you were plastered by the time we left the restaurant, because I did not want you to touch me.

The next day was too warm for you to wear your new boots, so you wore shorts and sandals. I wore the turquoise pendant with light linen pants and a loose top.

"Don't forget your cane," you said when we were about ready to go.

Wouldn't think of forgetting it, you ass.

"I've got it right here, sweetie. Have you got your camera?"

"Why would you ask such a stupid question?" you barked, and I knew phase two had begun.

Butter her up, then bring her down.

Chimayo was as charming as ever, and you had a hard time glaring at me over the festive table, alive with colorful ceramic plates. I knew I was supposed to be stricken with anxiety, and should ask you, with desperation, what was wrong, but instead I ordered another glass of Sangria and flan for dessert.

"Sweetie, are you sure you won't have some?" I asked, knowing it was one of your favorites.

"No, and I want to get out of here now. I want to take some pictures of the gorge and the light should be about right."

You slapped down your credit card, scribbled a tip on the bill, and got up and walked out without offering to give me a hand. The waiter gave you a dirty look and moved the heavy wood chair so I could scoot out.

We drove in silence, as was our custom when I was on your shit list, to the bridge that crossed the

Rio Grande. You pulled off the road and parked in a gravel lot.

Stepping out of the car, you ignored me completely, tucked your hearing aids in your shirt pocket, picked up your camera, and walked to a rugged pathway that ran along the edge of the gorge.

I got out of the hot car, assessed the terrain, and cautiously followed, using the cane for balance. By the time I caught up, you were poised on a ledge, intensely absorbed with your camera, and oblivious to my approach.

I looked at you standing so straight, still perfect posture, tight butt, great legs. I held the cane horizontally in my left hand. I may not have been able to run much, but my once skinny arms were now toned and strong.

One mighty whack across the back of your knees was all it took. Your legs buckled and your camera flew out of your hands. Off balance, you made a grab for it and over you went.

Down and down, 600 feet into the flowing waters. In movies, people always scream when they are falling, but I heard nothing, just the rush of the water and the stirring of a slight breeze.

I was numb as I picked my way back through the shale to get to the car. I couldn't call for help if I sounded like I was placing an order for Chinese take-out, so I sat and thought about every mean, cruel, demeaning thing you had done to me. Then I thought about what once had been, and what could have been.

The tears burst forth with the thunder of the Seven Sisters Falls, and the 911 operator could scarcely understand what I was telling her through my sobs.

A slew of helpers arrived. Sheriffs' cars, a truck-type vehicle identified as First Responders Unit, an ambulance and eventually a helicopter. A woman Sheriff's deputy sat with me in the car, and it was all a haze. A paramedic gave me a pill, some sort of sedative, to quell my sobs and shaking enough so that I could tell them what happened.

"He took his camera and walked over there to take some pictures. I guess he got so involved with getting the right shot, he forgot how close he was to the edge, and he leaned over too far, and—oh God, it's so awful—he fell over." The flood of tears began again.

Please, please believe me.

"And where were you when he fell?"

"Just sitting here in the car, watching him. I can't walk on uneven surfaces, even with my cane. He left the keys so I could turn on the air conditioner if I got too hot. He was always so kind, so considerate." Flood.

"Was he drinking or on meds?" the kind deputy asked, patting my hand.

"No. He had one beer with lunch at Chimayo an hour or so ago, but that was all. He was perfectly healthy, and my whole heart went over that ledge with him. I can't believe this. He was my life."

More flood.

She drove me in her patrol car to an Urgent Care facility in Santa Fe, and a doctor prescribed another sedative. Someone drove the rental car back to the timeshare, and when the deputy and I arrived there, she asked if there was anyone who could stay with me.

"No, but I'll call my best friend in California, and she'll know what to do."

Her cell rang, and there was a muffled conversation. The deputy sat down beside me, took my hand, and said, "They've retrieved your husband's body. It was quite a way down river, and it's lucky we found it before nightfall. Do you think you could make the identification now, or would you rather wait until tomorrow?"

"I want to do it now, to get it over with. This isn't real, is it?" I asked. She drove us to the coroner's facility, and we waited for your body to arrive. They had wrapped you in sheets, and only your face was visible. The second sedative had taken hold, and I was able to nod that it was you without too much of a flood.

"There will be a routine autopsy, and then the remains will be available for disposal. Do you know what he wanted?" she asked.

Years before, I had (over your objections until you realized I was paying) bought us each a plan with the Neptune Society, the expensive one, where they take care of everything no matter where you are when you croak. I explained this to the deputy and told her I would contact Neptune tomorrow.

"You'd better give them a call tonight, because sometimes things move quickly, and it works better if it's all set up. You can sign a form now, if you want, authorizing us to release the body to them."

"Yes, that's good," I said and signed. The deputy drove me back to the timeshare, gave me her card, and told me she would call me tomorrow to see if I needed help from Social Services. I thanked her profusely, collapsed on the couch, and made the three phone calls I knew I had to make. It felt weird not having you around.

First, the Neptune Society. I specified a cremation, a cheap container, and it was to be mailed to me in California.

Second, your daughter. That started two floods, but she said she would notify the rest of your family. She knew you wanted a cremation, but I should feel free to dispose of the ashes as I saw fit.

Third, Josie. "You really did it? And with one whack? I am so fucking proud of you. That bastard tortured you for almost ten years. I kept thinking shit, now I'll have to go to the anniversary party and eat his damned spaghetti. Get back here fast."

The next day, I called the deputy, choked as if I were holding back tears, and told her I was flying back to California where I had people to help me.

"Take care, dear. We all feel for you."

*   *   *

The cardboard box of ashes arrived about three weeks later, and a separate container held your wedding ring, your drowned watch, and the gold bracelet I had given you as a wedding gift.

Republic Waste Disposal comes every Thursday, at about 10:30 am, sending two trucks to empty separate garbage and recycle containers, so Wednesday night I was careful to place you in the garbage bin, because, God knows, I didn't want you coming back.

Thursday morning, I watched from the upstairs office window, surrounded by huge black plastic bags stuffed with your clothing and shoes waiting for pickup by the Salvation Army.

The garbage truck was right on schedule, lumbering and clattering down the street with its iron claws grabbing each container and upending it into the grinder, and it finally got to you. A crunch as the jaws closed, a thump as the contents of the container were tipped into the machine.

So you were roasted and freshly ground, just the way you liked your coffee.

Arrivederci, my love.

Acknowledgements

I thank the California Writers Club, Mt. Diablo Branch, for enabling this neophyte author to access wonderful support: Lyn Roberts, creative editor and superb coach/cheerleader, Ellen Barrons, scrupulous copy editor, enthusiast Robin Gigoux who introduced me to a Friday afternoon coterie, chock full of talented, encouraging writers and Andrew Benzie, publisher and magician. Thank you all.